AGAIN!

To Louis Pascal

A Red Fox Book

Published by Random House Children's Books
20 Vauxhall Bridge Road, London SW1V 2SA

A division of The Random House Group Ltd
London Melbourne Sydney Auckland
Johannesburg and agencies throughout the world

3 5 7 9 10 8 6 4

First published in Great Britain by The Bodley Head Children's Books 2000

Red Fox edition 2001

Printed in Hong Kong

THE RANDOM HOUSE GROUP Limited Reg. No. 954009

www.randomhouse.co.uk

ISBN 0 09 940415 X

AGAIN!

JOHN PRATER

RED FOX

It was a lovely sunny day and Grandbear was enjoying the warm
sunshine, when a little voice said, "Play with me, play with me."
It was Baby Bear, and Baby Bear wanted to play.

So Grandbear climbed
out of the hammock,

and together they
built a tower out of
Baby Bear's bricks.

Baby Bear pushed them over.
CLATTER!
CRASH!

"AGAIN!"
said Baby Bear.

So they built
an even bigger
tower of bricks,

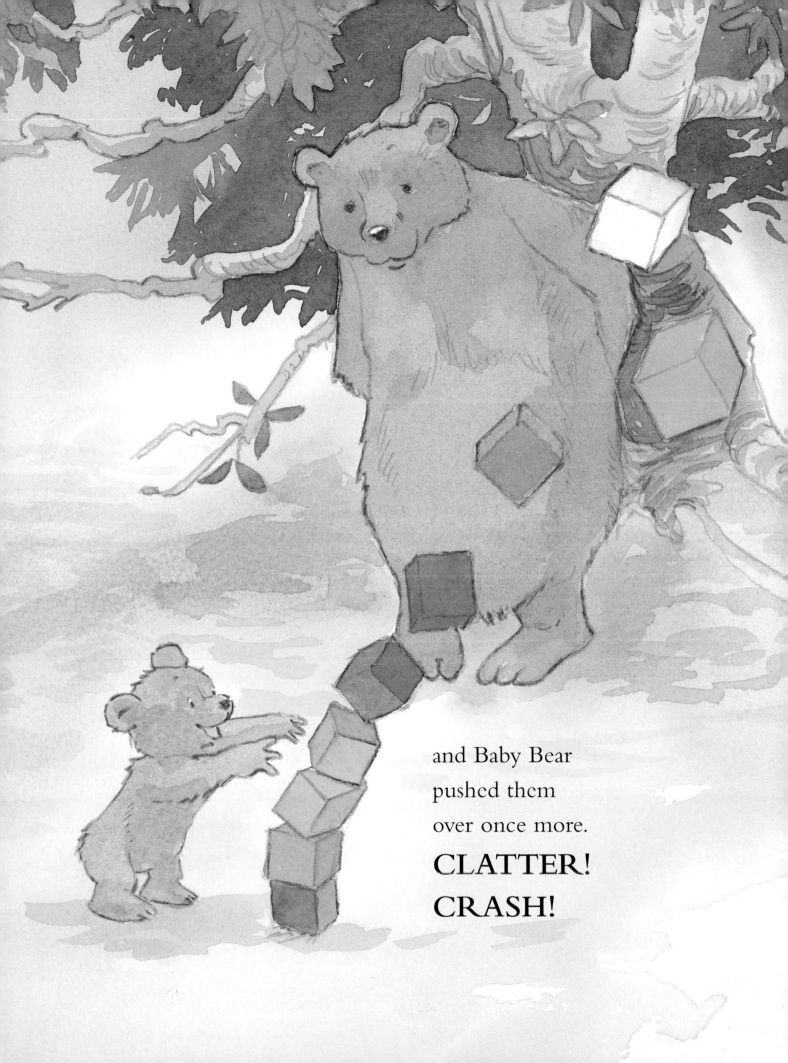

and Baby Bear
pushed them
over once more.
CLATTER!
CRASH!

"AGAIN!" said Baby Bear.
"Are you sure?" asked Grandbear,
who was getting a bit tired of
this game.
"AGAIN!" said Baby Bear.

So together they built
the biggest tower they
could using all the bricks.

Baby Bear pushed them all over for a third time.
CLATTER! CRASH!

"AGAIN!" said Baby Bear.
"No," said Grandbear, "let's do
something else."

They went over to the sandpit,
and with a little help from Grandbear,
Baby Bear made a sandcastle.

Baby Bear had great
fun stamping it down.
STAMP! STOMP!

"AGAIN!"
said Baby Bear.

So they filled the bucket
lots of times, and made
a big sandcastle.

This took a lot of stamping down.

STAMP! STOMP!

"AGAIN!" said Baby Bear.
"Are you sure?" asked
Grandbear who was
getting very tired of
this game by now.
"AGAIN!" said
Baby Bear.

So they filled the bucket lots and lots of times until they had
made the biggest sandcastle ever.

And what did Baby Bear do?

"**AGAIN!**" said Baby Bear.
"No, no," said Grandbear.

"Let's do something useful. Let's water the plants."

So Grandbear filled
the watering-cans,
and they watered
the smallest plants.
PLIP! DRIP!

The watering-cans
were soon empty.

"AGAIN!"
said Baby Bear.

Grandbear filled the watering-can again, and Baby Bear watered the bigger plants. DRIP! DROP!
"AGAIN!" said Baby Bear.

Then, using the hose, Baby Bear watered
the biggest plants. **DRIP! DROP!**
"AGAIN!" said Baby Bear when Grandbear
turned off the tap.

"No, no, no," puffed Grandbear.
"You've watered everything.
Let's do something else."
Grandbear made a cold
drink, and found Baby
Bear's biggest
and best story-book.

Then together,
they clambered
into the hammock.

Grandbear read the story all the way through from beginning to end.
"AGAIN!" said Baby Bear.

But Grandbear's eyes were beginning to close.
Baby Bear gave Grandbear a kiss and a cuddle.
"Again," murmured Grandbear, sleepily.
And so Baby Bear hugged Grandbear again...

and again...

       and again.